"Jack," whispered Annie. "I think the ninjas know we're here."

Jack peeked over the windowsill of the tree house. His eyes met the dark eyes of the tall ninja on the ground.

"*E-hy!*" the ninja cried. He dashed toward the tree. The other ninja followed.

"Oh no!" said Annie.

"We've got to go!" Jack said. "Where's the Pennsylvania book?"

He and Annie looked around wildly.

But where was the book about Pennsylvania? Jack and Annie couldn't get home without it!

First Stepping Stone Books you will enjoy:

By David A. Adler
(The Houdini Club Magic Mystery series)
Onion Sundaes
Wacky Jacks

By Kathleen Leverich
Brigid Bewitched
Brigid Beware!

By Mary Pope Osborne
(The Magic Tree House series)
Dinosaurs Before Dark (#1)
The Knight at Dawn (#2)
Mummies in the Morning (#3)
Pirates Past Noon (#4)
Night of the Ninjas (#5)

By Barbara Park
Junie B. Jones and Some Sneaky Peeky Spying

By Louis Sachar
Marvin Redpost: Alone in His Teacher's House

By Marjorie Weinman Sharmat
Genghis Khan: A Dog Star Is Born
Genghis Khan: Dog-Gone Hollywood

By Jerry Spinelli
Tooter Pepperday

By Camille Yarbrough
Tamika and the Wisdom Rings

Magic Tree House #5

Night of the Ninjas

by Mary Pope Osborne

illustrated by Sal Murdocca

A FIRST STEPPING STONE BOOK

Random House 🏠 New York

For Penn Sultan

Library of Congress Cataloging-in-Publication Data
Osborne, Mary Pope. Night of the Ninjas / by Mary Pope Osborne ;
illustrated by Sal Murdocca
p.   cm. — (The Magic tree house series ; #5) "A First stepping stone book."
SUMMARY: The magic tree house takes Jack and Annie back in time to feudal
Japan where the siblings learn about the ways of the Ninja.
ISBN 0-679-86371-0 (pbk.) — ISBN 0-679-96371-5 (lib. bdg.)
[1. Time travel—Fiction. 2. Ninja—Fiction. 3. Japan—Fiction.]
I. Murdocca, Sal, ill. II. Title. III. Series: Osborne, Mary Pope.
Magic tree house series ; #5.
PZ7.081167Ni 1995 [Fic]—dc20 94-29142

Manufactured in the United States of America
10 9 8 7 6 5 4 3 2 1

Random House, Inc. New York, Toronto, London, Sydney, Auckland

Contents

Prologue

One summer day in Frog Creek, Pennsylvania, a mysterious tree house appeared in the woods.

Eight-year-old Jack and his seven-year-old sister, Annie, climbed into the tree house. They found that it was filled with books.

Jack and Annie soon discovered that the tree house was magic. It could take them to the places in the books. All they had to do was to point to a picture and wish to be there.

Jack and Annie visited the time of dinosaurs, old England, ancient Egypt, and a pirate ship.

Along the way, they discovered that the tree house belonged to Morgan le Fay. Morgan was a magical librarian from the time of King Arthur. She traveled through time and space, gathering books.

Jack and Annie are about to start a whole new adventure...in *Night of the Ninjas*.

1

Back into the Woods

"Let's look again, Jack," said Annie.

Jack and Annie were walking home from the library. The path went right by the Frog Creek woods.

Jack sighed. "We looked this morning," he said. "We looked the day before. And the day before that."

"Then you don't have to come," said Annie. "I'll go look by myself."

She took off into the woods.

"Annie, wait!" Jack called. "It's almost

3

dark! We have to get home!"

But Annie had disappeared among the trees.

Jack stared at the woods. He was starting to lose hope. Maybe he would never see Morgan again.

Weeks had passed. And there had not been one sign of Morgan le Fay. Nor had there been one sign of her magic tree house.

"*Jack!*" Annie called from the woods. "*It's back!*"

Oh, she's just pretending as usual, Jack thought. But his heart started to race.

"Hurry!" called Annie.

"She better not be kidding," said Jack.

He took off into the woods to find Annie.

Night was falling fast. Crickets chirped

loudly. It was hard to see through the shadows.

"Annie!" Jack shouted.

"Here!" she called.

Jack kept walking. "Here *where?*" he called back.

"Here *here!*"

Annie's voice came from above.

Jack looked up.

"Oh man," he breathed.

Annie waved from the window of a tree house. It was in the tallest oak in the woods. A long rope ladder hung down from it.

The magic tree house was back.

"Come on up!" Annie shouted.

Jack ran to the rope ladder. He started climbing.

He climbed and climbed and climbed.

As he climbed, he looked out over the woods. High above the treetops it was still light.

At last, Jack pulled himself into the tree house.

Annie sat in the shadows. Books were scattered everywhere.

On the floor the letter M glowed in the dim light. The M stood for Morgan le Fay.

But there was no sign of Morgan herself.

"I wonder where Morgan is," said Jack.

"Maybe she went to the library to get some more books," said Annie.

"We were just at the library. We would have seen her," said Jack. "Besides, the library's closed now."

Squeak!

A little mouse ran out from behind a stack of books. It ran to the M shining in the floor.

"Yikes," said Annie.

The mouse sat on the middle of the M. It looked up at Jack and Annie.

"Oh, it's so cute," Annie said.

Jack had to admit the mouse was cute. It had brown-and-white fur and big dark eyes.

Annie slowly reached out her hand. The mouse didn't move. Annie patted its tiny head.

"Hi, Peanut," she said. "Can I call you Peanut?"

"Oh brother," said Jack.

"Do you know where Morgan is?" Annie asked the mouse.

Squeak.

"You're nuts, Annie," said Jack. "Just because the mouse is in the tree house doesn't mean it's magic. It's a plain old mouse that crawled in, that's all."

Jack looked around again. He saw a piece of paper on the floor.

"What's that?" he said.

"What's what?" asked Annie.

Jack went over and picked up the paper. There was writing on it.

"Oh man," whispered Jack, after he read the words.

"What is it?" said Annie.

"A note," said Jack. "It must be from Morgan. I think she's in big trouble!"

2

The Open Book

Jack showed Annie the piece of paper. It said:

Help me - Under a spell
Find 4 thin

"Oh no," said Annie. "We have to help her. But what's a *thin?*"

"Maybe she was trying to write *things*," said Jack. "See how the *n* sort of runs off the page?"

"Maybe the spell was starting to make her disappear or something," said Annie.

"Right," said Jack. "I wonder if she left any other clues." He glanced around the tree house.

"Look!" Annie pointed at a book in the corner. "That's the only open book," she said.

Jack looked around again. Annie was right. He felt a shiver go down his spine.

Jack went over to the book and picked it up. He held it near the window. Light from the setting sun was golden on the page.

Jack stared at the picture on it. In the picture were trees with white flowers. The trees were on the side of a mountain. Near a wide, rushing stream.

Two people were also in the picture. They wore dark clothes. They had black scarves over their faces. And long swords strapped to their backs.

"Oh man," whispered Jack.

"Who are they?" Annie asked.

"Ninjas, I think," said Jack.

"Ninjas? Really?" said Annie.

"Morgan must have left the book open to this page for a reason," said Jack.

"Maybe that's where she was when the spell got her," Annie said.

"Or maybe that's where the four things are," said Jack.

"Let's go!" said Annie.

"Now?" said Jack.

"Yes, Morgan's in trouble! She needs us *now!*" said Annie.

"But we should read this book first," said Jack. "So we'll be prepared."

"Forget it!" said Annie. "Every minute counts!" She grabbed the book from Jack.

"Give it back," he said. "We have to find out about this place."

Annie held the book out of reach. "We'll find out when we get there," she said.

"We don't even know where *there* is!" Jack said.

But Annie pointed at the picture. "I wish we could go here," she said.

The leaves of the oak tree began to shake.

Squeak!

"Don't be scared, Peanut," said Annie. She scooped up the mouse. Then she put it in the pouch of her sweatshirt.

The wind began to blow.

It blew harder and harder.

The tree house started to spin.

Faster and faster!

Jack squeezed his eyes shut.

Then everything was still. Absolutely still.

Except for the sound of rushing water.

3

E-hy!

Jack opened his eyes.

Annie was already looking out the window. The mouse peeked out of her pouch.

Jack looked out the window, too. The air was fresh and cool.

The tree house was in a tree with white flowers. The tree was in a grove of trees on the side of a mountain. Nearby a wild stream rushed downhill.

Two ninjas were standing on rocks near the water. They were staring at the valley below.

One ninja was tall. The other was short. They wore black pants and shirts. They had black scarves around their heads. And swords strapped to their backs.

It was exactly like the picture in the book.

Jack crouched below the window.

"Be careful," he whispered. "Don't let them see you."

"Why not?" Annie whispered back.

"They might think we're some kind of enemy," said Jack quietly.

Annie crouched beside him.

Jack pushed his glasses into place. *Now* he was going to look at the ninja book.

He picked up the book. He turned to the beginning. He read:

> Very little is known about the shadowy warriors called ninjas. Historians believe that ninjas

lived in Japan between the 14th and 17th centuries. Both men and women were ninjas. Sometimes they fought to protect their families. Sometimes warlords hired them to be spies.

"Wow," whispered Jack. "We're in Japan, hundreds of years ago."

Jack opened his backpack. He pulled out his notebook and pencil. He liked to take notes. He wrote:

ninjas were warriors in old Japan

"Jack," whispered Annie. "They're looking up. I think they know we're here."

Jack peeked over the windowsill. His eyes met the dark eyes of the tall ninja.

"*E-hy!*" the ninja cried. He dashed toward the tree. The other ninja followed.

"Oh no!" said Annie.

"We've got to go!" Jack said. "Where's the Pennsylvania book?"

He and Annie looked around wildly.

But where was the book about Pennsylvania? It had the picture of the Frog Creek woods in it. Jack and Annie couldn't get home without it.

"It's not anywhere!" cried Annie.

"We've got to do something. Fast!" said Jack. "Pull up the ladder!"

He and Annie grabbed the top of the rope ladder. They pulled the ladder into the tree house.

But the tall ninja leaped at the tree trunk. Then he started climbing up the tree! The short ninja followed. They climbed just like cats!

Jack and Annie huddled in a corner.

The ninjas climbed into the tree house. Neither one made a sound.

4

Captured

The ninjas pulled iron bands off their hands. The bands had spikes like claws on them.

"That's how they climbed the tree," Annie whispered to Jack.

The ninjas stared at Jack and Annie with dark, piercing eyes. The rest of their faces were covered by their scarves.

Jack felt frozen under their stares.

Annie wasn't frozen, though. She stepped right up to them.

"Hi," she said.

The ninjas didn't say "hi" back. They didn't move at all. They were as still as Jack.

"We're trying to help our friend, Morgan," said Annie.

She held up Morgan's note.

The tall ninja took the note from her. He looked at it. Then he gave it to the short ninja.

The two ninjas stared at each other. Then they looked back at Jack and Annie.

Finally the short ninja nodded once. He put the note into the pocket of his shirt.

"You can help us?" Annie asked.

Neither ninja spoke. Jack wished he could see their faces. He couldn't tell what they were thinking.

The short ninja tossed the rope ladder back out of the tree house. The tall one pointed down the ladder. Then he pointed at Jack and Annie.

Uh-oh, thought Jack. Were they being captured?

"Us? Go with you?" said Annie.

The ninja nodded.

"Oh boy!" said Annie.

Oh boy? Is she nuts? wondered Jack.

The short ninja darted down the ladder. He went hand over hand. His feet didn't touch the rungs of the ladder.

The tall one did the same.

Jack gasped. The ninjas moved very fast. They were like spiders dropping from webs.

"Wow!" said Annie.

"Now's our chance to leave," said Jack. "Quick!" He looked around the tree house again. Where *was* that Pennsylvania book?

"Let's go with them, Jack," said Annie.

"No! This isn't a game!" Jack said.

"But I think they know something about Morgan!" said Annie.

She started down the ladder.

"Come back!" said Jack.

But it was too late.

Jack sighed. "Why does this *always* happen?" he asked himself.

"Come on, Jack!" came Annie's voice from below.

Jack put his notebook and the ninja book into his pack. He pushed his glasses into place. And he started down the ladder.

Jack joined Annie and the ninjas on the ground.

The sun had fallen behind the hills. The

sky was streaked with red and gold.

The mouse peeked out from Annie's sweatshirt pouch.

"Don't be scared, Peanut," Annie whispered. "We'll take care of you."

Great, thought Jack. *But who is going to take care of us?*

The short ninja held Jack's arm in one hand and Annie's arm in the other. He led them through the twilight. The tall ninja walked behind them.

"Where are we going?" Jack asked.

The ninjas stopped near the rushing water of the wide stream. The water roared as it raced downhill.

The short ninja looked at Jack and Annie. He let go of their arms. Then he pushed them toward the stream.

"You want us to cross it?" shouted Annie.

The ninja nodded. Then he and the short ninja stepped into the wild stream. They started wading across.

"Let's run back to the tree house!" said Jack.

"No, we have to follow them!" said Annie. "For Morgan's sake!"

Jack took a deep breath. She was right.

Annie grabbed Jack's hand. Together they stepped into the water.

"YIKES!" They both screamed and jumped out.

It was the coldest water Jack had ever felt! It was colder than ice. It was so cold it felt like fire.

"I can't go back in," said Annie, shivering.

"Me neither," said Jack. "I'll have a heart attack."

The ninjas looked at Jack and Annie. Then

they turned around and came back.

The tall ninja grabbed Jack.

"Help!" Jack cried.

But the ninja lifted Jack high into the air.
And put him on his shoulder.

The short ninja put Annie on his shoulder.

Then the two ninjas stepped into the stream again. The icy wild waters swirled around them. It went up to the short ninja's waist.

But the ninjas moved through the stream as calmly as two sailing ships.

5

Flames in the Mist

The water grew shallow again. Then they were on dry land. The ninjas lowered Jack and Annie to the ground.

"Thanks," said Annie.

"Thanks," said Jack.

Squeak, said the mouse.

The ninjas said nothing, but they looked around.

Jack looked around, too. A full moon was rising in the sky. Dark rocks dotted the side of the mountain.

Then the ninjas started moving. They

went silently up the slope, between the rocks.

Jack and Annie followed them. Jack wasn't afraid of the ninjas now. In fact, he was starting to like them. Maybe they really could help find Morgan.

The ninjas moved silently. But Jack and Annie made plenty of noise.

They panted as they climbed the rocky hillside. Their wet sneakers made squishy sounds.

Suddenly the ninjas froze. Jack could see their eyes darting around. Voices were coming from the valley below. Jack saw torches flaming in the mist.

The ninjas started moving faster. Jack and Annie hurried after them.

"Who's carrying the torches?" Annie asked.

Jack was too out of breath to speak. He also didn't have an answer.

They came to a pine forest. Night birds called out. Wind rattled the branches.

The ninjas moved like ghosts through the forest. They appeared and disappeared, through moonlight and shadows.

Jack and Annie struggled to keep up.

Finally the ninjas came to a stop.

One ninja held out his hand, as if to say, *Wait.* Then both ninjas stepped away into the shadows of the trees. And were gone.

"Where did they go?" said Annie.

"I don't know," said Jack. "Maybe the book can tell us."

He pulled the ninja book out of his pack.

He turned the pages until he came to a picture of a cave.

By the light of the full moon, he read:

> Sometimes ninjas held meetings in
> hidden mountain caves to plan
> secret missions.

"Oh man," said Jack, "I bet they went inside a hidden cave."

He pulled out his notebook and pencil. He wrote:

meetings in hidden caves

Jack turned the page. He stared at a picture of a ninja sitting on a mat. He read:

> Ninjas took orders from a ninja
> master. The master was a mysteri-
> ous wise person who knew many
> secrets of nature.

"Wow," whispered Jack.

Just then the two ninjas returned. Jack quickly put his books away.

The short ninja motioned for Jack and Annie to follow. In the shadows was the entrance of a dark cave.

"What's in there?" Annie whispered.

"The ninja master," Jack whispered back.

6

Shadow Warrior

Jack and Annie went into the cave. They followed the ninja through the darkness.

The back of the cave was lit with dozens of candles. Shadows danced on the walls.

In the flickering light, Jack saw a dark figure sitting on a woven mat.

The ninja master.

The ninja bowed to the master. Then he stepped to one side.

The master stared at Jack and Annie.

"Sit," he said.

Jack and Annie sat on the cold, hard floor.

Squeak.

The mouse poked its head out of Annie's pouch.

"It's okay, Peanut," said Annie.

The master stared at the mouse for a moment. Then he looked at Jack. "Who are you?" he asked.

"I'm Jack and that's my sister, Annie," Jack answered.

"Where do you come from?" the master asked.

"Frog Creek, Pennsylvania," Annie answered.

"Why are you here?" he asked.

"We're trying to help our friend Morgan le Fay," said Jack. "She left us a message."

Annie pointed to the short ninja. "We gave the message to him."

"You mean, you gave the message to *her*," said the ninja master. "And *she* has given it to me."

"*She?*" said Jack and Annie together.

The woman ninja's eyes sparkled. Jack thought she might be smiling.

The master held up Morgan's note.

"Perhaps I can help you," he said. "But first you must prove yourselves worthy of my help."

Just then the tall ninja appeared. He made a sign to the master.

The master stood up. He handed Morgan's note to Annie.

"We must go now," he said. "The samurai are close."

"Samurai?" said Jack. He knew that the samurai were fierce Japanese fighters.

"Were they the ones in the valley?" Jack asked. "The ones with the torches?"

"Yes, our family is at war with them," said the master. "We must leave before they find us."

"But what about helping Morgan?" said Annie.

The master strapped on his sword.

"I have no time now," he said. "I must go."

"Can't we go with you?" said Annie.

"No, there is no place for you where we

are going. You must find your way back to your house in the trees."

"Alone?" said Jack.

"Yes. You must go alone. And beware of the samurai."

"Why?" said Jack.

"They will think you are one of us," said the master. "They will ask you no questions. They will show you no mercy."

"Yikes," whispered Annie.

"But you have seen the way of the ninja. You can practice it yourselves now," said the master.

"H-how?" said Jack.

"Remember three things," said the master.

"What?" said Jack.

"Use nature. Be nature. Follow nature."

"I can do that!" Annie said.

Jack looked at her. "You can?" he said.

The master turned to Jack. "Your tree house lies to the east. That is the way you must go," he said.

How? wondered Jack. *How do we find the east?*

Before he could ask, the master bowed. Then he disappeared into the shadows.

The two ninjas led Jack and Annie out of the cave, into the moonlight.

The tall one pointed at the pine forest. Then they too disappeared into the darkness.

Jack and Annie were all alone.

7

To the East

Jack and Annie stood still for a long moment.

Annie spoke first. "Well, I guess the tall ninja was pointing to the east," she said. "I guess that's the way we go."

"Wait," said Jack. "I need to write some stuff down."

He took out his notebook. In the moonlight, he wrote:

1. use nature
2. be nature
3. follow nature

"Look, Jack," whispered Annie. "Do I look like a ninja?"

He looked at her. She had pulled her sweatshirt hood over her head and tied the strings tightly.

She did look like a ninja—a very small one.

"Good idea," Jack whispered. He pulled his hood up, too.

"Okay, let's go," said Annie.

Jack put his notebook away. Then he and Annie headed east into the woods.

They slipped between trees. And more trees. And more trees.

All the trees looked the same. Jack got confused. Were they still going in the right direction?

"Wait," he said.

Annie stopped. They both stared at the woods around them.

"Do you think we're still going east?" asked Jack.

"I guess so," said Annie.

"We can't just guess," said Jack. "We have to know for sure."

"How do we do that?" said Annie. "We don't have a compass."

Just then the master's words came back to Jack.

"The ninja master said to *use nature*," he said.

"How do we do that?" said Annie.

"Wait, I remember something—" Jack closed his eyes.

He remembered something in a camping book. *Now what was it?*

He opened his eyes. "I've got it! First we need a stick," he said.

Annie picked up a stick. "Here—" she said.

"Great, now we just need a space with moonlight," said Jack.

"There—" said Annie.

They moved into a moonlit space between the shadows.

"Now push the stick into the ground," Jack said.

Annie pushed the stick into the ground.

"The stick's shadow looks like it's more than six inches," said Jack. "What do you think?"

"It looks like it," said Annie.

"Okay. Then that means the shadow's pointing east," said Jack.

"Neat," said Annie.

"So *that way* is east!" Jack pointed to a

new direction. "At least I hope it is."

"We're real ninjas now!" said Annie.

"Yep," said Jack. "Maybe we are. Come on!"

They took off—heading east, they hoped.

Soon they were out of the pine woods and walking down the rocky mountainside. They moved slowly from rock to rock. Finally they rested against a giant rock.

"Let's check our direction again," said Jack.

Annie stuck another stick into the dirt.

"There," he said. He pointed to the shadow on the ground. "That way—"

Annie peeked over the rock, down the mountain.

"Yikes," she said softly.

Jack looked, too. His heart nearly stopped.

There were flames of fire coming up the mountain. The samurai!

Jack and Annie ducked behind the rock.

Squeak, said the mouse.

"Quiet, Peanut," said Annie.

Jack reached into his pack. He pulled out the ninja book.

"I hope something in here can help us," he said.

Jack flipped through page after page until he found what he was looking for. It was a picture of warriors wearing bamboo armor. They were holding swords. He read:

> The samurai were fierce Japanese fighters. They carried two swords to cut down their enemies.

Annie tapped Jack on the shoulder.

Jack looked at her.

She pointed up the mountain.

A figure was coming down toward them. He was very near.

In the moonlight, his bamboo armor was shining. His two swords were gleaming.

It was a samurai warrior!

8

Dragon Water

Jack and Annie crouched together. Samurai were on both sides of them now. They were trapped!

Jack pressed against the rock.

The warrior stepped closer and closer. He looked to the right. He looked to the left.

Jack held his breath.

"*Be nature,*" whispered Annie.

"What?" Jack whispered back.

"*Be nature.* Be a rock."

Oh brother, thought Jack. This was nuts.

But he squeezed his eyes shut. Then he tried to be part of the rock.

Jack tried to be as still as the rock. As solid as the rock. As quiet as the rock.

Soon he started feeling as strong as the rock. As safe as the rock. He wanted to be the rock forever.

Squeak.

"He's gone," said Annie. "They're all gone."

Jack opened his eyes. The samurai warrior was gone. Jack stood up and looked over the rock. The torches were gone, too.

"Let's go," Annie said.

Jack took a deep breath. He felt great—he was getting more and more like a ninja every minute. Maybe even like a ninja master.

"East!" he said.

And they went east. Down the mountain, between the rocks. Until they came to the wide, icy stream.

The water seemed even wilder than before.

"I don't see the tree house," said Annie.

Jack looked across the stream to the dark grove of trees. Moonlight shone on their pale flowers. But where was the tree house?

"I don't see it either," said Jack. "We have to cross the water first. Then we'll try and find it."

The water was crashing and rushing over the rocks.

Squeak. The mouse peeked out from its pouch.

"Don't be afraid," said Annie. She patted

the mouse's little head. "Be like us. Be like a ninja, too."

"Let's go," Jack said.

He took a deep breath and stepped into the stream. The icy water swirled up to his knees. The current knocked him over.

Jack grabbed some weeds. He held on tight as water swirled around him.

He was freezing to death!

"Jack!" Annie grabbed Jack's arms. She helped him back onto the bank.

"That was close!" said Annie.

Jack wiped his glasses. Luckily, they hadn't fallen off in the water.

"Are you okay?" said Annie.

"N-not really," said Jack, his teeth chattering. He was chilled to the bone.

"We'll never get across," said Annie.

"We'll drown if we try."

"Or fr-freeze to death," said Jack.

He pulled off the hood of his sweatshirt.
He didn't feel much like a ninja anymore.

Annie pulled off her hood too. She sighed.
"What can we do?" she said.

Squeak.

Peanut climbed out of Annie's sweatshirt pouch and leaped onto the ground.

The mouse scampered away.

"Peanut, come back!" Annie called.

"No," said Jack. "We have to follow Peanut."

"Why?" asked Annie.

"We have to do what the master said!" said Jack. *"Follow nature!"*

"Oh. Right!" said Annie. "Follow Peanut! But where is Peanut?"

In the moonlight Jack saw the little mouse. It was running through the grass along the stream.

"There!" he cried. "Come on!"

Annie hurried after Jack. Jack hurried after Peanut. They ran beside the rushing waters.

A moonlit branch had fallen across a narrow part of the stream. It touched both shores.

The mouse was running over the branch.

"Peanut's going over a bridge!" said Annie. She started to follow.

"Wait!" cried Jack. "We can't go on that branch. It's too small! It'll break!"

9

Mouse-walk

The mouse vanished into the tall grass on the other side of the stream.

Jack and Annie stared at the tree branch.

"We have to *try* to cross it," said Annie. "We're supposed to follow nature."

"Forget it," said Jack. "It's too little. It'll crack in a second."

"Maybe if we pretend we're mice, we can do it," said Annie.

"Oh brother," said Jack. "Not again."

"If you could be a rock, you can be a mouse," said Annie. "Just be teeny and light and fast."

Jack took a deep breath.

"We *have* to," said Annie.

"Okay," Jack said.

"Say 'squeak,'" said Annie.

"You're nuts!" said Jack.

"Just do it," said Annie. "It'll help you feel more like a mouse."

Jack groaned. "Okay," he said. "Squeak."

"Squeak," said Annie.

"Squeak, squeak, squeak," they said together.

"Let's go! Hurry!" said Annie.

Jack stepped onto the branch.

I'm teeny. I'm light. I'm fast, he thought. Then he darted across the branch.

Jack moved so quickly, he didn't think about anything—except getting to the other side.

He forgot the wild, freezing water. He forgot the smallness of the branch.

Suddenly Jack was on the other side. Suddenly Annie was right beside him.

They laughed and fell together into the grass.

"See! See! The branch didn't break!" said Annie.

"I guess it was big enough," said Jack. "I guess we just had to think the right way."

"The Peanut way," said Annie.

"Yeah," said Jack, smiling. He felt great.

He was still wet from his fall into the stream. But he didn't mind anymore.

Jack pushed his glasses into place and stood up. "Okay, now we just have to find the tree house," he said.

"No, we don't," said Annie. She pointed up.

The tree house was outlined against the

moonlit sky. High in a tree. Surrounded by white flowers.

In the distance came the sound of voices. Then Jack saw flames.

"The samurai are coming back," said Jack. "We have to go."

"Where's Peanut?" said Annie. "We can't leave Peanut."

"We have to," said Jack.

The voices of the samurai were getting closer. So were their torches.

"Come on," Jack said. He grabbed Annie's hand. He pulled her toward the rope ladder.

"Oh Jack—" she said sadly.

"Go! Go!"

Annie started up the rope ladder.

Jack followed. He felt sad, too. He liked that little mouse now. He liked it a lot.

They climbed up and up.

Just before they got to the top, Jack heard it.

Squeak.

"Oh wow!" cried Annie. "Peanut's inside!"

Annie pulled herself into the tree house. Jack followed.

He gasped.

Someone else was in the tree house, too.

A dark figure was sitting in the corner.

"You have done well," the figure said.

It was the ninja master.

"You have followed the way of the ninja," he said.

"Oh man," breathed Jack.

Squeak.

The master was holding Peanut.

"Take good care of your little helper," he said, handing the mouse to Annie.

Annie kissed the mouse's tiny head.

"And take this—" said the master. He held his hand out to Jack.

He gave Jack a small, round stone.

"This moonstone will help you find your missing friend," the master said.

Jack stared at the stone. Was this one of the four things?

"You must go home now," said the master. He picked up the Pennsylvania book and handed it to Annie.

"Where did you find it?" asked Jack.

"Here," said the master. "You did not see it before. Because your heart knew you had a mission to complete first."

"What about you?" said Annie. "Can you come with us?"

"Yes," said Jack. "We need help finding Morgan."

The master smiled. "No, my friends. I

must stay here. There will be more help along the way. But you must find the way on your own."

Annie opened the book. She found the picture of Frog Creek.

She pointed to it. "I wish we could go there," she said.

The wind started to blow.

The white flowers started to shake. Clouds covered the moon.

"Remember," the master said, "keep a kind heart."

Then he swung silently down the rope ladder. He disappeared into the dark night.

"Wait!" Jack called. There was so much he wanted to ask the master. About nature. About ninjas. About their mission.

But the tree house started to spin.

It spun faster and faster!

Jack gripped the stone in his hand. He squeezed his eyes shut.

Then everything was still.

Absolutely still.

10

'Night, Peanut

Jack opened his eyes.

Then he opened his fist. He stared at the moonstone in his hand. It was clear and smooth. It almost seemed to glow.

"We're home," said Annie.

Squeak.

Annie and the mouse were looking out the window.

Jack looked with them.

The sun was setting in the distance.

No time at all had passed in Frog Creek.

They heard their neighbor's dog, Henry, bark. They heard crickets chirping.

In the distance, they could see their dad step out of their house. He stood on their porch.

"Ja-ack! An-nie!" he called.

Time for dinner.

"Com-ing!" Annie shouted.

Jack sat back on his heels. He looked at the moonstone again.

"I guess we have one of the four things," he said.

"We'll look for the other three tomorrow," Annie said.

Jack nodded. They had a lot more work to do.

He put the moonstone in his pocket.

He pulled on his pack.

"Ready?" he said.

"Wait," said Annie. She took off one of her sneakers. She pulled off her sock. Then she put her sneaker back on.

"What are you doing?" said Jack.

"I'm making a bed," she said.

"A what?"

"Bed! You know, for Peanut to sleep in." Annie picked up the mouse. She tucked it inside her sock.

"'Night, Peanut," she said softly.

Squeak.

"Oh brother," said Jack.

Annie held the mouse close to Jack.

"Kiss it goodnight, Jack," she said.

"Don't be silly," he said. "Let's go."

"Thanks for helping us," Annie said to the mouse.

She put Peanut gently down on the glowing M. She pulled Morgan's message out of her pouch. And put it next to the mouse.

"See you tomorrow," she said. Then she started down the ladder.

Jack stared at the mouse. It looked back at him.

For a moment, its dark eyes looked old and wise.

"Come on, Jack!" called Annie.

Jack kissed its tiny head.

"Night-night, Peanut," he whispered.

Then Jack headed down the rope ladder.

It got darker and darker as he went down.

By the time he stepped onto the ground, it was almost completely black.

"Where are you?" said Jack.

"Here," said Annie. Her hand bumped his. He took it.

"Careful," he said.

"Careful yourself," she said.

Together they took off through the cool, dark woods.

They moved silently and swiftly—two shadow warriors returning home.

The Magic Tree House is back!

Join Jack and Annie
as they travel through time
in another exciting story by
Mary Pope Osborne.

Look for Magic Tree House #6
Afternoon on the Amazon
in Fall 1995!

Read the first four
Magic Tree House books
by Mary Pope Osborne

Magic Tree House #1, DINOSAURS BEFORE DARK,
in which Jack and Annie discover the tree house and
travel back to the time of dinosaurs.

Magic Tree House #2, THE KNIGHT AT DAWN,
in which Jack and Annie go to the time of knights
and explore a medieval castle with a hidden passage.

Magic Tree House #3, MUMMIES IN THE MORNING,
in which Jack and Annie go to ancient Egypt and get
lost in a pyramid when they help a ghost queen.

Magic Tree House #4, PIRATES PAST NOON,
in which Jack and Annie travel back in time and meet
some unfriendly pirates searching for treasure.

About the Author

Mary Pope Osborne is an experienced time traveler. As a kid, she and her brothers used to pretend the picnic table was a ship that could take them anywhere. Now she writes books that carry her (and her readers!) through time and around the world. "I would rather have a magic tree house," she says, "but I can't find one big enough for everyone I want to take with me."

She and her husband, Will, live in New York City and spend their weekends in Pennsylvania.